This book belongs to

....

....

Useful words

(in the order they appear in this book)

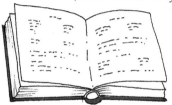

cookbook

cake

butter

bowl

sugar

Easter eggs

milk

spoon

flour

flowers

tin

oven

wand

table

candles

Too many cooks!

Katie Carr

Bouncy Ben was looking at

a cookbook.

"It's Clever Cat's birthday today,"

he said to Sammy Snake.

"Let's make a cake for her."

Best Biscuits
Baking Buns
Book Birthday
cakes

"What do we need?" asked
Sammy Snake.

"Butter," said Bouncy Ben,
blending some butter in a big bowl.

"Something sweet," said Sammy,
putting some sugar into the bowl.

Birthday Cake
2 eggs
250g flour
100g butter
100g sugar
vanil
Mix
and su

sugar

"Every cake needs eggs,"
said Eddy Elephant.

"We don't need Easter eggs,"
cried Bouncy Ben.

"The book just says eggs ...,"
said Sammy. But it was too late!

"We need milk," said Munching Mike. "Let's put in some metal, too," he said, dropping the spoon in as well.

"No!" cried Bouncy Ben.
But it was too late!

"We need flour," said Fireman Fred.

"I have some pretty flowers," said Golden Girl as she flung them into the bowl.

"Wait!" cried Sammy Snake. But it was too late!

Quarrelsome Queen looked into the bowl.

"That's not a cake," she said crossly. "It's a mess! You must put it right quickly. Clever Cat will be here soon."

"We need to mix it," said Max and Maxine.

They mixed and mixed, but the cake mixture was still a mess.

"We need to bake it," said Bouncy Ben, bringing a tin. He tipped the cake mixture into the tin.

Then Sammy Snake slid the tin into the oven. They all had to wait for the cake to cook.

"Look out!" shouted Quarrelsome Queen, as Bouncy Ben went to open the oven.

"That tin is hot. Let me help," said Lamp Lady. She took the cake out of the oven and put it on a little table.

Ticking Tess tasted the cake. "It tastes terrible," she said. "Oh dear, what shall we do?"

"We need the Water Witch," said Sammy Snake. "She can wave her wand and save the cake."

The Water Witch waved her
wand. Quick as a wink the
mess was turned into a big
birthday cake.

"Just in time," said Bouncy Ben.
"Here comes Clever Cat."

"Thank you," purred Clever Cat. "I can see that you have all been very busy. But there is just one thing missing ..."

Then with another wave of her wand, the Water Witch put candles on top of the cake!

The Letterlanders

Annie Apple	Bouncy Ben	Clever Cat	Dippy Duck	Eddy Elephant	Fireman Fred	Golden Girl

Hairy Hat Man	Impy Ink	Jumping Jim	Kicking King	Lucy Lamp Lady	Munching Mike

Naughty Nick	Oscar Orange	Poor Peter	Quarrelsome Queen	Robber Red	Sammy Snake	Ticking Tess

Uppy Umbrella	Vase of Violets	Wicked Water Witch	Max and Maxine	Yo-yo Man	Zig Zag Zebra

This edition produced for
The Book People Ltd., Hall Wood Avenue,
Haydock, St. Helens WA11 9UL

Published by Collins Educational
An imprint of HarperCollins*Publishers* Ltd
77-85 Fulham Palace Road
London W6 8JB

© Lyn Wendon 1998

First published 1998
Reprinted 1998

ISBN 0 00 3033805

LETTERLAND® is a registered trademark of Lyn Wendon.

The author asserts the moral right to be identified as the author of
this work.

British Library Cataloguing in Publication Data
A catalogue record for this book is available from the British Library.

Written by Katie Carr
Illustrated by Maggie Downer
Designed by Michael Sturley
Consultant: Lyn Wendon, originator of Letterland

Printed by Printing Express, Hong Kong